MEL BAY'S GETTING INTO.......
FIDDLING
by CRAIG DUNCAN

CD Contents

1	Boil Them Cabbage Down	21	Orange Blossom Shuffle	41	Maggie Brown's Favorite
2	Old Joe Clark	22	Reuben's Train	42	The Blarney Pilgrim
3	Cottoneyed Joe	23	Salt River	43	Miss McLeod's Reel
4	Devil's Dream	24	Bill Cheatham	44	The Girl I Left Behind Me
5	Fire on the Mountain	25	Katy Hill	45	The Rakes of Mallow
6	Soldier's Joy	26	Sally Johnson	46	Red Haired Boy
7	Liberty	27	Sally Goodin'	47	Guilderoy83
8	Arkansas Traveler	28	Westphalia Waltz	48	St. Anne's Reel
9	Eighth of January	29	Jolie Blonde	49	Temperence Reel
10	Whiskey Before Breakfast	30	Ashoken Farewell	50	Flowers of Edinburgh
11	Cripple Creek	31	Faded Love	51	Drowsy Maggie
12	Sailor's Hornpipe	32	Maiden's Prayer	52	Pigeon on the Gate
13	Turkey in the Straw	33	Irish Washerwoman	53	Scotland the Brave
14	Fisher's Hornpipe	34	Swallow Tail Jig	54	The Salamanca Reel
15	Blackberry Blossom	35	Garry Owen	55	Harvest Home
16	Down Yonder	36	Kesh Jig	56	The Rights of Man
17	Ragtime Annie	37	Haste to the Wedding	57	Gentle Maiden
18	Billy in the Lowground	38	Morrison's Jig	58	Fanny Power
19	Back Up and Push	39	Merrily Kiss the Quaker	59	Sheebeg, Sheemore
20	Rubber Dolly	40	The Road to Lisdoonvarna		

1 2 3 4 5 6 7 8 9 0

Visit us on the Web at www.melbay.com — E-mail us at email@melbay.com

Alphabetical Listing of Tunes

Bicycle Built for Two (3/4 time)

```
D...|...|...|...
Daisy, Daisy,
G...|...              D...|...
give me your answer do
A...|...   D...|...
I'm half crazy,
E7...|...            A...|...
all for the love of you
  A...|...            D...|...
It won't be a stylish marriage
  Bm7...|...    A...|...
I can't afford a carriage
      D...       A...   D...      A...
But you'll look sweet, upon the seat
      D...   A...    D...|...
Of a bicycle built for two
```

Table of Contents

Introduction

This book presents a working fiddlers repertoire in a variety of styles. Old time and bluegrass tunes include ideas for variation and improvisation. Celtic and Irish tunes have appropriate ornamentation suggested. A wide variety of fiddling techniques are explained and used throughout the book. After working through this text, the player should be able to attend a fiddle jam session and play with confidence.

The approach to fiddling is quite different from the approach to violin playing. The bowing in general is connected, very relaxed and free flowing. The left hand is also relaxed, occasionally bending notes, and doubling fourth finger and open strings. Vibrato is also relaxed and slower. Most fiddlers today can read music to some extent, however, they rarely do in performance. They usually memorize melodies and play the sounds and improvisations they hear in their head.

Is it harder to play the violin or the fiddle? First of all, not all fiddlers play "violin" nor all violinists "fiddle." The major contractor of recording violinists in Nashville, Tennessee once warned a new hotshot violinist, "Don't think you can go out and compete with the fiddlers in this town, they're too good." I've known violinists who could sight read anything you put in front of them, but couldn't improvise a note, and when they did read transcriptions of fiddle music sounded too stiff. I've also known world class fiddlers who don't read music. So, the answer to the question, "is it harder to play the violin or fiddle," is yes. It is best to give great respect to all styles of playing the instrument.

Acknowledgements

Special thanks go to Bill Bay for the many opportunities to write about fiddling for Mel Bay Publications. Thanks to Jim Prendergast for his recording services and guitar work in producing the CD that accompanies the book. Thanks also goes to you, the fiddling public, who haved purchased and continue to purchase these books aimed at preserving the integrity of great fiddle music.

So, is it a fiddle or a violin?

"Are you playing a fiddle or a violin?" "What is the difference between a violin and a fiddle?" "Aren't they really the same instrument, just played differently?" All violinists and fiddlers have heard questions like these.

We have also heard many answers. "A violin has strings, and a fiddle has strangs." "A violin sings and a fiddle dances." "A violin is like an opera singer and a fiddle is like a country singer." "They're the same instrument, just played in a different manner." Actually, all of these questions and answers are valid.

Consider the names *violin* and *fiddle*. Merriam Webster's Collegiate Dictionary describes a violin as "a bowed string instrument having four strings tuned at intervals of a fifth..." The definition given for fiddle is, "violin." The World Book Encyclopedia describes the violin as "the best known and most widely used of all string instruments," and goes on to say they were first built around 1500. Under fiddle, the encyclopedia states, "see violin." So it seems that they really are the same instrument. Why the two names? There were other stringed instruments built in the 1500's and 1600's, and some of these were called fiddles. They were bowed instruments, with slightly different construction, and the number of strings could vary. As time passed, and the art of instrument making improved, the violin became the main bowed instrument held on the shoulder. Although classical composers and musicians used the name violin, other musicians, particularly folk musicians, continued to call their instruments fiddles. That practice continues today. People will usually refer to the violin as the instrument used in symphony orchestras, in classical music and in "high brow" performances. Likewise, the term "fiddle" usually refers to the instrument used for country music, celtic music and other forms of folk and improvised music. Despite the common association with different styles of music, the terms have become quite interchangable. I have heard many "violinists" (musicians who play classical music) refer to their instruments affectionately as their "fiddle." It is also common to hear fiddlers (musicians who play bluegrass, Irish or some other form of folk music) call their instruments "violins."

Although they really are the same instrument, there are differences to be discussed. The tone quality of violins can vary greatly from instrument to instrument, and different tones are desirable for different styles of music. A concert violin soloist needs an instrument that sounds very brilliant, with a great deal of projection, to be heard above an orchestra. On the other hand, a fiddler needs an instrument that has a very warm tone, that will blend well in smaller settings. Fiddlers often play through microphones, both in live and in recording situations. The very characteristics of brilliance and projection needed by the symphony player may sound very "nasal" or "pinched" through a microphone placed close to the instrument. Although it is possible to find one instrument that is great in all circumstances, it is more likely that using different instruments for different styles of music will give the best results. If you only have one instrument, don't be discouraged by this discussion of tone. Play what you have!

The set up of an instrument will also affect its sound and playability. It has been said that fiddlers use "flat" cut bridges and steel strings while violinists use "round" cut bridges and gut strings. There is some truth in this, but it is not altogether accurate. Most players experiment with different strings until they find what works best on their instrument. This is true regardless of style. I know many fiddlers who use gut or synthetic gut strings and have also seen violinists use steel strings. As far as bridge cut is concerned, that is pretty standard among most players. I personally have a Sam Zygmantowicz violin set up with *Tomastik Dominant* strings for classical, string quartet music and string section recording; and I have a Natale Carletti Italian violin set up with *D'Addario Helicore* heavy gauge strings for fiddle music and close microphone recording. The bridge cut is the same. I have tried many possibilties of strings and set ups and will vary the choice of instruments as needed. I have used my "fiddle" in a chamber ensemble when I wanted a warmer sound and my "violin" in a Celtic band when I wanted to be as loud as the accordion.

So, is it a fiddle or a violin? The answer is yes. The instrument is called by both names and can be used in many styles of playing in many genres of music. Remember the encyclopedia says it is "the best known and most widely used of all string instruments."

Boil Them Cabbage Down

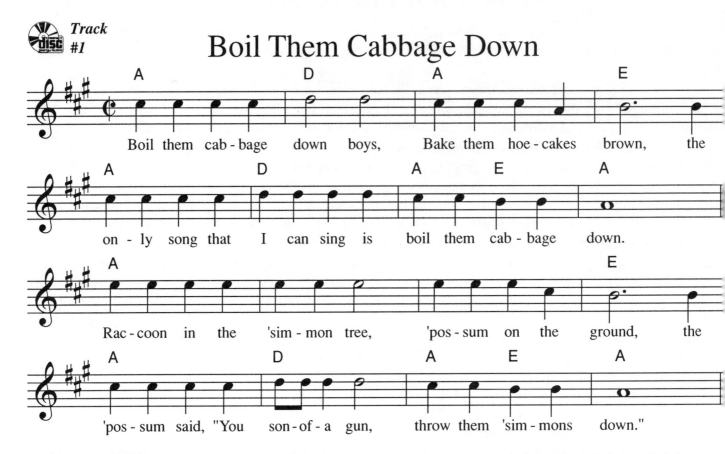

This is a very basic old time "fiddle song." The first eight measures are the chorus and the second eight are the verse. The fiddlers job is to play or "fiddle" the melody. Playing the melody exactly as written will sound very stiff, so fiddlers have developed many techniques to give the music more life, or make it more fun.

One of the most commonly used techniques to give a melody a sense of rhythm comes from the square dance tradition. It uses a repeated bowing pattern of quarter - eighth - eighth. This is called *shuffle bow*. Another commonly used practice is to repeat each section of a tune. The following fiddle solo on *Boil Them Cabbage* uses the shuffle bow and repeats each section.

6

Another fiddling technique is using double stops. This variation uses the shuffle bow, repeats, and double stops. Notice that the fourth finger and the open E are played together in the third line. This doubling of fourth finger and the open string is common through out fiddling.

Adding notes around the melody is another way of "fiddling" a tune. Notice that the melody note is found on the first beat of each measure of this variation. The shuffle bowing pattern is also used, by slurring the moving notes to continue a quarter - eighth - eighth bowing rhythm, even though the notes change. This gives a strong driving beat to the tune.

Old Joe Clark

Above is the basic melody of *Old Joe Clark*. Although the fiddler should play the melody, it needs to be presented in a more interesting style. This variation uses the shuffle bow and adds a few notes around the melody.

The following variation begins with the fourth finger on the A string doubling the open E. There are more notes added around the melody, yet the shuffle bowing pattern stays constant until the end of the phrase. Notice that the fourth measure of the B part goes to an E chord instead of a G chord. Old time fiddlers usually play an E at this part of the tune, while bluegrass musicians usually use a G.

Track
#3

Cottoneyed Joe

This is a very popular tune which is used for a dance of the same name. The first part is eight measures long and is usually repeated. The second part is really only four measures long, but includes a written variation to make it eight measures long. This version uses a combination of shuffle bowing and other bowing.

This variation starts with a down bow slur into the downbeat. This happens several times through the tune and gives a different lilt to the tune by breaking the monotony of the constant shuffle bowing. Fiddlers use a variety of bowing techniques. Much of fiddle music is dance music, so the bowings are used to emphasize the rhythm. Combining different bowings while still underlining the rhythm adds interest to a tune.

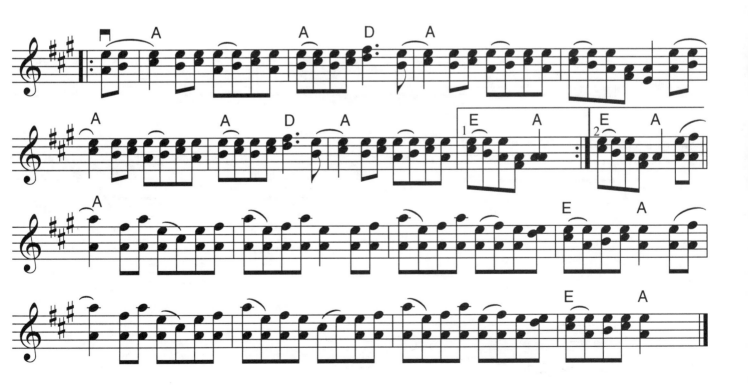

Devil's Dream

This is a favorite tune among violinists who are learning to fiddle, because it is played with more of a violinist approach than a hoedown fiddler approach. The bowing is "saw stroke," in other words, each note is played with a separate bow stroke. The bow should be placed on the string so that the right forearm is parallel to the ground. Very short strokes should be used, no more than an half inch long. The string crossings in the third and fourth measures, and in the first four measures of the B part, should be done with the wrist only. A good way to learn this technique, is to hold something lightly between the right elbow and side, such as a cassette box, while practicing the string crossings using only the wrist.

Here are two variations you can add to your version of Devil's Dream. The first one requires shifting to third position for the high C♯ and B. Notice the last two measures of these two variations are different from the last two measures of the parts presented above. Both endings are common to the tune.

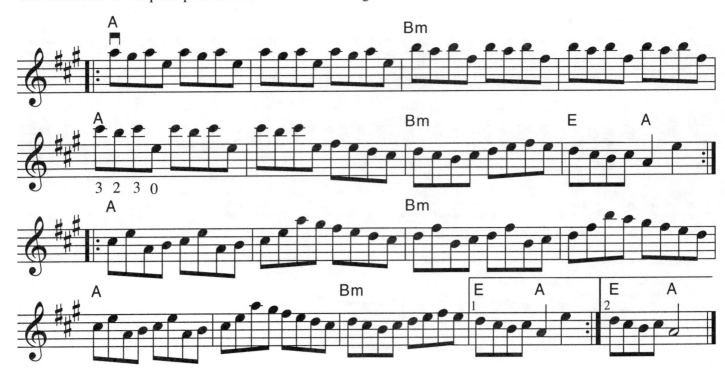

Track #5

Fire on the Mountain

Bluegrass and old time fiddlers often play this tune. It is an American melody that is performed at a very fast tempo. It is a very repetitive melody which uses the shuffle bowing to create a driving rhythm. When using this bowing, be careful not to accent the slurred notes (which fall on the beat). Practice playing every note evenly, so that there is no accent at all. After you can do this, practice accenting the offbeat (the first eighth note after each slur). Fiddlers often accent the offbeat when playing driving tunes such as this one.

An unusual quirk about this tune is the "extra" two measures at the end, making the B part ten measures long, instead of eight. Because of these extra measures, this does not make a good square dance tune, but it is a very good "show" tune when played up tempo.

The following arrangement uses the melody above (with only one slight variation) played with the adjacent open string. The bow should remain evenly on the two strings, allowing the fingering to imply the melody.

Soldier's Joy

This is a very old tune played by many American fiddlers. It is presented here with the standard melody using shuffle bowing.

The bowing can be changed in the first part to emphasize the open A strings played on the beat. This gives the music a strong accent on the beat. Slurring notes to accommodate string crossings is a common fiddling technique.

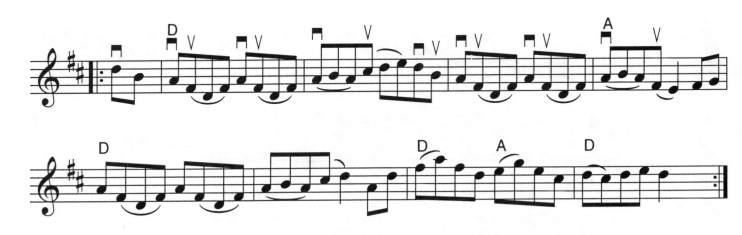

Old time fiddlers often play *Soldier's Joy* with fewer notes than the original melody, much like an old time banjo player. The following examples are in this style, using open drone strings, shuffle bowing and cross string bowing.

Liberty

This American fiddle tune is played by many old time and bluegrass fiddlers. Although the second part is often played with more notes, the simple beauty of the melody is presented here.

Liberty is a favorite tune to play with "twin" fiddles. The "twin" part is usually the parallel harmony above the melody.

Harmony part

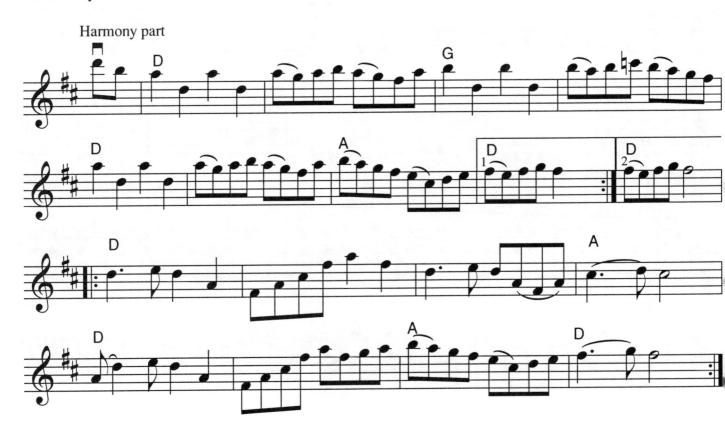

Arkansas Traveler

This is a two part American fiddle tune. The first part is played in the low octave using shuffle bowing and open strings as drones. The second part is played in the high octave with a bow styling called *Georgia Bow*. This technique uses a down bow on the off beat, followed by up bow slurs on the next three eighth notes. It gives a very rhythmic effect to the music and is used in old time and Cajun fiddling.

Lines 5 and 6 are a high octave variation on the A part. The bowing in the third measure of line 5 emphasizes the beat by using a down bow on the E string followed by up bows on the notes played on the A string. Lines 7 and 8 are a low octave drone style variation on the B part. The last line uses the first two and last two measures of the tune as a tag.

15

Eighth of January

This traditional American tune was written to honor the American victory in the Battle of New Orleans on January 8, 1814. The shuffle bowing is used here to give an old time square dance feel to the tune.

This variation starts with a typical fiddling lick, that guitar players would refer to as a" hammer-on". It is common for fiddlers to play the note below the melody note and slur up, or hammer-on, to the melody note. The B part in this variation uses the fourth finger on the D string in unison with the open A string.

Jimmy Driftwood wrote a famous song entitled *The Battle of New Orleans* based on this melody. To play the song in a better singing range, transpose the tune to the key of G by moving everything over one string, beginning with an open D string instead of an open A string.

16

Whiskey Before Breakfast

This old time tune has become a favorite of many fiddlers and guitarists. It is a two part tune, played with many interpretations of the two parts. Old time fiddle tunes often have specific outlines as to where the melody goes, without defining each note literally. The first version presented here is a standard statement of the melody.

The first part of the tune in this variation is played in the high octave. Bowings in tunes like this one are open to interpretation. This example starts with a "saw stroke" and also uses "shuffle bow." It would also be stylistic to incorporate "Georgia bow" (see page 15) in the third, fourth, seventh and eighth measures

Fiddle tunes can vary in accompanying chord selection as well as in note selection. The second part in this variation has an A chord which is not in the variation above.

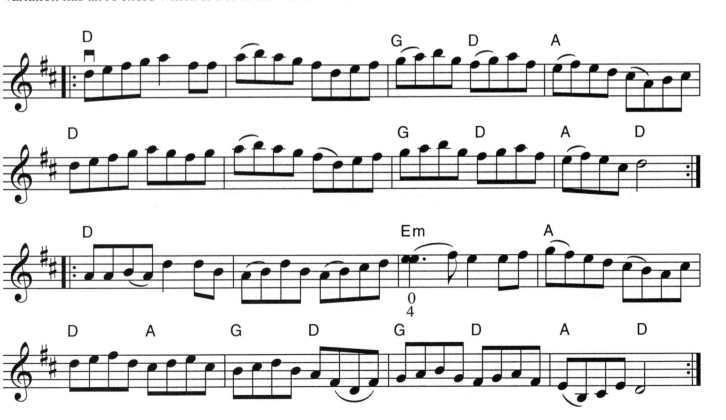

17

Cripple Creek

I got a girl and she loves me, She's as sweet as sweet can be,

She's got eyes of ba-by blue, Makes my heart beat strong and true.

Go-in' up Crip-ple Creek, go-in' in a run, Go-in' up Crip-ple Creek to have some fun.

Go-in' up Crip-ple Creek, go-in' in a whirl, Go-in' up Crip-ple Creek to see my girl.

Almost every banjo player knows this old time tune, therefore, fiddlers need to know it also. The melody in the third and fourth measures is interchangeable with the melody in the seventh and eighth measures. Here is a variation incorporating the higher melody (She's as sweet as she can be) in measures three and four.

The A part in this variation uses the lower melody (Makes my heart beat strong and true) found in measures 5-8 of the vocal. The B part has slides indicated on the B notes. These pitches are to be started flat and raised to pitch, never going sharp. The pressure on the bow and left finger is released while the left forefinger moves down for the second slide upward. This movement back to the flatted pitch is not to be heard.

Cripple Creek is played in the key of A as well as in the key of G. The licks in the two keys vary slightly as the fiddler will use string crossings and note choices that fit best in the respective key. The first variation here is a very typical approach to this tune in the key of A.

Slides are used in the B part of this variation. They should be heard only as the note is started slightly flat and is raised up to pitch.

Sailor's Hornpipe

Musicians from many backgrounds know or at least have heard this tune. The bowings indicated are only suggestions to make the tune flow smoothly.

Sailor's Hornpipe is also played in the key of A. The notes in the second measure have been changed to make the tune work better in this key.

Turkey in the Straw

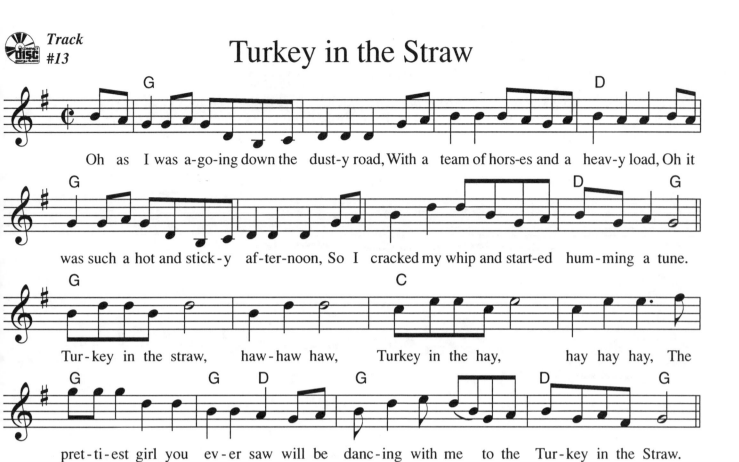

Oh as I was a-go-ing down the dust-y road, With a team of hors-es and a heav-y load, Oh it was such a hot and stick-y af-ter-noon, So I cracked my whip and start-ed hum-ming a tune. Tur-key in the straw, haw-haw haw, Turkey in the hay, hay hay hay, The pret-ti-est girl you ev-er saw will be danc-ing with me to the Tur-key in the Straw.

Also known as *Old Zip Coon*, this American tune has become a standard in the fiddler's repertory. Because of it's familiarity, it is often requested. Although the melody presented above is correct for the vocal, fiddlers usually play a more embellished version. Shuffle bowing is used in the following arrangement to give an old time square dance feel to the tune.

21

Fisher's Hornpipe

This is the original key of *Fisher's Hornpipe*. The melody here dates back to printed versions in the nineteenth century. Although this version is authentic, modern fiddlers often play the same notes in the third measure as are written in the second measure. An example of this is in the following arrangement in the key of D.

The third part found here is not original to the tune. It can be traced back as far as a 1920's era recording of Eck Robertson. Notice that the final four measures are the same as the last four measures of the second part.

It has become common practice to play *Fisher's Hornpipe* in the key of D. This version attempts to present the original melody along with typical phrasing used by old time and bluegrass fiddlers. Notice that the second and third measures use the same notes and chord changes. This is different from the original tune.

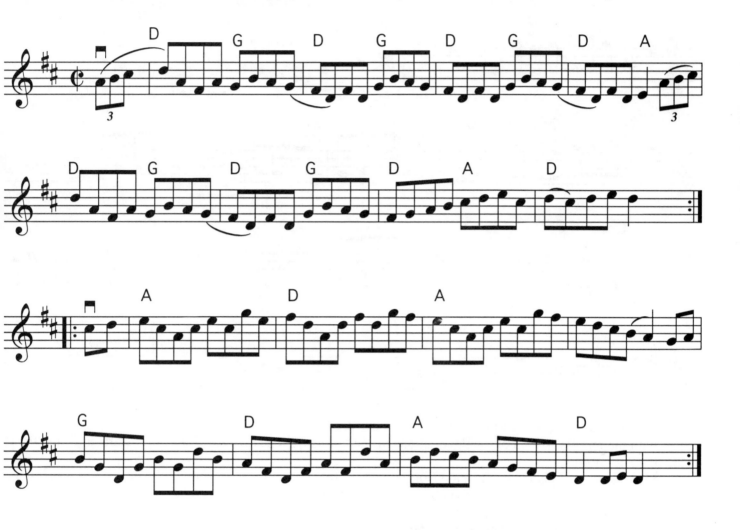

This is the optional third part in the key of D. Remember that it is not part of the original tune and is not played by all fiddlers.

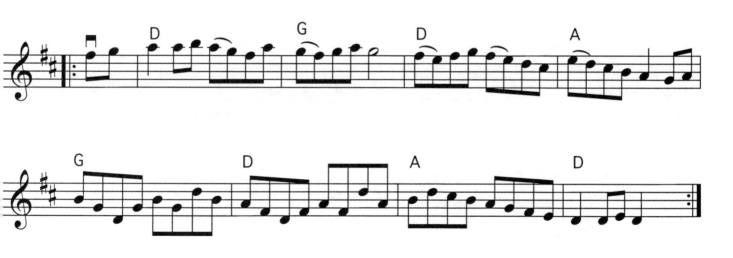

Blackberry Blossom

Fiddlin' Arthur Smith from Tennessee wrote this two-part tune which has become a favorite among old time and bluegrass fiddlers. This is the basic melody.

Following is a theme and variation arrangement of Blackberry Blossom. Keep in mind that this is a two-part tune, with the repeats written out with variations instead of using repeat signs. The A part starts in G and the B part starts in E minor.

The first A part uses both shuffle and Georgia bow to create more rhythmic interest. The second A part is in the low octave. Be certain to follow the bowings in the third A part on the descending triplets.

The last four measures are a tag using the descending scale pattern found in the first A part.

A common variation on the chords is found in the first A part. The chords actually remain the same while the bass notes follow a descending scale pattern. This pattern may be used at the musicians' discretion.

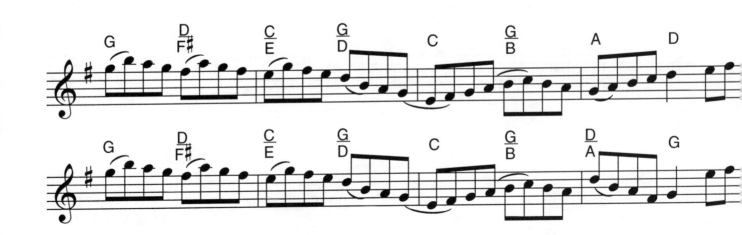

24

26

Down Yonder

Made popular by country pianist Del Woods, this tune is an instrumental favorite. When playing the tune with a band, the two measures marked echo are played by an instrument other than the lead. Here is the basic melody.

Several types of fiddle licks are used in this version of *Down Yonder*. Double stops introduce the tune. The fourth finger on the A string is used to double the open E string and rhythmic bowings emphasize string crossings. The slides up to the B naturals should be heard sliding upward only.

Ragtime Annie

Track #17

This traditional American tune, also called *Raggedy Ann*, begins with a rocking bow. It is important to follow the slurs marked in the first four measures to give the proper emphasis. The first section is repeated. The B part is not repeated.

The third part presented here is not commonly played by all fiddlers. However, it is a later addition to the tune, so it is worth including. I prefer to play the first two parts through several times and then play this part as a bridge section before returning to the first two parts to close the tune.

30

Billy in the Lowground

Old time, as well as contest and bluegrass fiddlers play this tune. It has two parts, and is a classic case of a tune having a basic outline of where it goes, but considerable freedom in the note choices in how it gets there. Bowing style is also very open. The first part here has the shuffle bowing indicated. The second part uses long bow, shuffle bow and another common bow lick found in the next to last measure. The pattern of three eighth notes slurred, followed by three eighth notes slurred, followed by two separate strokes is used in many tunes.

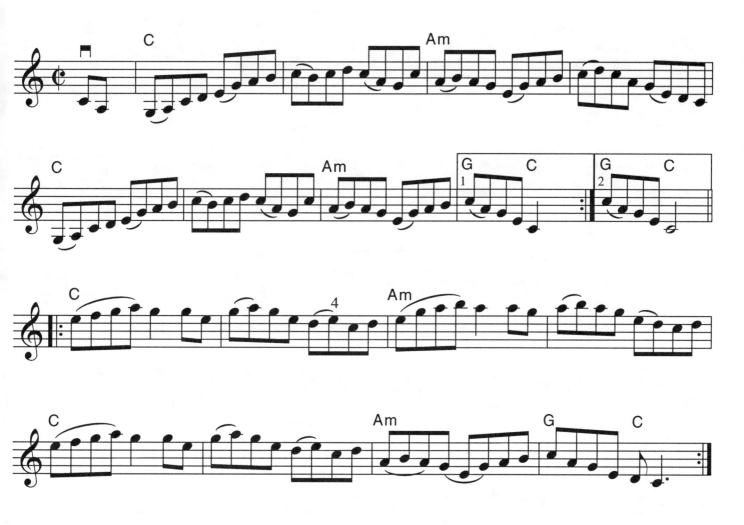

Here is another version of *Billy in the Lowground* with written variations instead of repeats. The A part uses mostly saw stroke bowing, though it still incorporates the three, three, one, one bow lick on the first two Am chords. The Am lick in the third line is played with the fourth finger on the D string doubling the open A.

The B part in this version uses an F chord in the third and fourth measures instead of an A minor. Although the A minor chord is more commonly used, many musicians use the F chord in the B part for tonal variety. By changing a couple of the F notes to E's, this variation will work with the substitution of the Am chord. The three, three, one, one bow lick shows up again in the fourth measure.

Double Shuffle Bowing

This bowing technique is used in many bluegrass, old time and show tunes including *Orange Blossom Special*. It is referred to negatively as "hokum bowing" and has been outlawed in many fiddling contests.

The pattern is sixteen notes long and is played on two or more strings. It begins down bow with two strokes on the lower string followed by one stroke on the higher string. This three-note pattern is played five times with the final stroke of the double shuffle being an up bow on the lower string.

Here is an example of the pattern on a C chord. Practice this repeatedly until you feel the rhythm it produces.

The sound of the double shuffle lick is often varied by changing the pitch of the higher string with each string crossing. In the following example the second and third fingers are alternated on the A string.

This exercise uses the double shuffle bowing as it changes back and forth between a C chord on the D and A strings, and a G chord on the A and E strings. Begin practicing this slowly, building up speed and accuracy.

Back Up and Push

This tune is played up tempo with a bluesy feel to the first part. The slide from the high B♭ to the A should be done with the fourth finger, moving the third finger out of the way. The E's on the A string should be played with the fourth finger and should "bend" slightly up to pitch. The second part of the tune is a classic use of the double shuffle bowing technique. This tune is often used as a jam tune, with "no holds barred" improvisation over the chords.

Rubber Dolly

Rubber Dolly is very similar to *Back Up and Push.* The first two lines written here state the melody of the tune. The third and fourth lines are a variation on this melody. The second part, lines 5-8, is a double shuffle variation on the chord changes.

Orange Blossom Shuffle

This exercise uses the chords found in the double shuffle part of *Orange Blossom Special.* Here is the section played on two strings. Practice this over and over until you can play the pattern automatically with very little pressure in your right arm.

Here is the same pattern played on three strings. It should be played with very short, smooth bow strokes, using only enough bow pressure to make the double stops sound. Practice this until you can play it in tune with as little effort as possible.

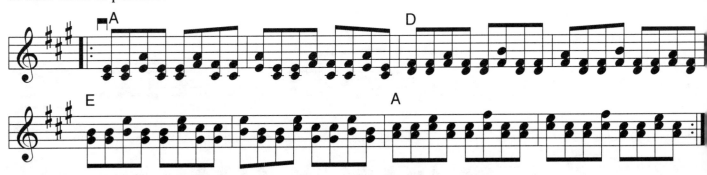

This is a variation on the *Orange Blossom Shuffle.* The section builds by beginning with a single shuffle bow pattern played across three strings, changing to the double shuffle in the seventh measure. When the second finger is used on the D string in the first two measures of the third line, and on the A string in the first measure of the fourth line, it remains on the string through the set of three notes. This technique is very common and should be mastered. The double shuffle ends in the last measure of the section with two half notes that act as a release.

Train Licks

Fiddles are sometimes used to imitate trains, and various tunes have sections dedicated to train sounds. Here are several examples of "train licks." Some are imitations of the train, others imply the momentum of the train, and others are just jamming licks.

This first lick imitates the train horn - "wooh-wooh." The B and G♯ should begin slightly flat and slide up to pitch and then back down as indicated. In the measures with the two down bows, the pressure on the bow and the left hand is released while the hand shifts backward, so that only the slides going up to pitch are audible. The same technique is applied in third position on the B and D, followed by a quick shift back to first position, sliding up to the G♯ and later down from the C♯ and E to the B and the open D.

Here are several more train whistle imitations, all based on inversions of the E7 or E9 chord. The pressure on the bow should be released at the end of the imitation, as the left hand slides flat, mimicking the sound of the train passing. All of these licks can be transposed to other keys by using the same inversions of the chords in the new key.

This is an imitation of the chugging of the train and the clacking of the tracks. The left hand notes the x's as indicated as the bow moves up and down the length of the strings, but still slightly across, making a percussive sound. The offbeats are accented. The left little finger is used to pluck the open E string, imitating the train bell.

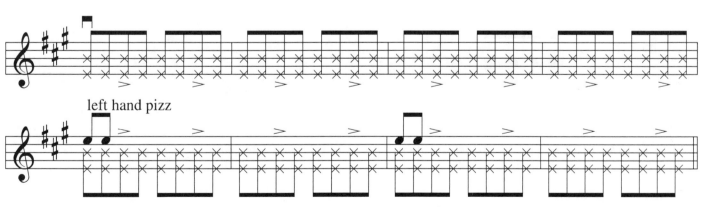

The *Orange Blossom Special* uses many of the techniques presented here. It is probably the most famous and widely played American fiddle tune, written in 1938 by Ervin Rouse and popularized first by fiddler Howard "Chubby" Wise. A full arrangement of the tune is found in the book, *Advanced Fiddling*, catalog number MB93971BCD, available at melbay.com or 1-800-863-5229.

Reuben's Train

This is an old time fiddle/banjo tune also known as *Lonesome Reuben*. When it is played by bluegrass banjo players in the key of B, it is called *Train 45*. This version uses open-string double stops to create the old time lonesome sound. The second part of the tune uses the flat seventh of the scale, C natural, to imitate the whistle of a train.

The techniques discussed on the Train Licks page can be used throughout this tune, including using the "chugging" imitation as a rhythmic backup lick. To do this, the left hand plays notes in a D chord as the bow moves up and down the strings.

Following is another variation on Reuben's Train. The first section is played an octave higher than in the previous version. The second part uses a C natural and an E over the D chord, producing train imitations on a D9 chord. The last line of the tune uses a lick that goes to a G chord. This phrase is usually played toward the end of the tune and is rarely played more than once in a full rendition.

Track #23

Salt River
Salt Creek

This old time fiddle tune has become a standard in the bluegrass fiddler's repertory. It has been recorded by many musicians including guitarist Doc Watson and is heard at many jam sessions. The two names for the tune are interchangeable, although bluegrass players tend to refer to it more often as *Salt Creek*. Here is a typical rendition of the two-part tune.

Here is an example of bluegrass style fiddling on this tune with the variations written out instead of repeats. The bowing is mostly shuffle, but uses other bow licks for rhythmic interest. The "push" (beginning the note ahead of the beat) from measure 8 to measure 9 using the fourth finger and open string is a very common fiddle lick. Be aware of changing between G sharp and G natural in the second part of the tune.

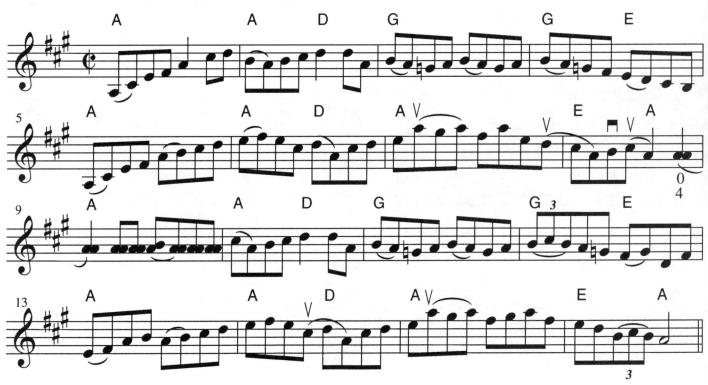

40

Track #24

Bill Cheatham

This is another standard among bluegrass and old time fiddlers, coming out of the Southern tradition of hard driving fiddle tunes. It is a two-part tune, played with many improvised variations. The basic melody of the first part is frequently played with double stops. The second part is played single note as the melody climbs through the A, D, E, A chord progression.

This is a one time through arrangement of *Bill Cheatham* offering several ideas for variations on the tune. The first eight measures are a typical single string statement of the first part. The lick in measures 9-12 comes from the fiddling of Vassar Clements. Be careful to play the C natural with a high first finger, so that the passage will flow. The second part of the tune begins in measure 17. The first time through is a rather typical variation. Measures 25-32 give a different twist, with the notes moving up in patterns of three.

42

Katy Hill

This tune is played by bluegrass and old time square dance fiddlers. It is a two-part tune, played up tempo. This is the basic form of the melody, but it will vary slightly from fiddler to fiddler. *Sally Johnson* is practically the same tune, played slower in a Texas contest style.

Using a four string G chord in the first part is such a common variation that it is included here. Notice also that the ending lick of the A part is different. The B part follows the same basic outline as the B part above.

43

Sally Johnson
Texas Contest Style Fiddling

This is practically the same tune as *Katy Hill*, but is played in a slower, fancier Texas contest style. The chord changes indicated are in the contest/western swing accompaniment style. The tune will also work over the simple changes found in *Katy Hill*. Bowing in the contest style uses quite a bit of saw stroke (changing bow direction with each note) and consciously avoids the use of shuffle bow and the double shuffle. Texas style contest fiddlers use fancy left hand fingerings and licks to make the music exciting, creating many variations. They play the tunes slower, from 100-120 beats per minute, usually with a slight swing. Old time square dance fiddlers use rhythmic bowing such as the shuffle bow and Georgia bow to create a driving excitement, playing at faster tempos from 112-144 beats per minute.

The first part of *Sally Johnson* is measures 1-8 with a written variation for the repeat in measures 9-16. Half step licks such as the B and Bb's in measure 1 and 3 are common in this style fiddling. The D# in measure 4 should be played with the fourth finger and the following E as an open string. The bow lick in measures 9 and 11 comes from the first part variation of *Katy Hill* (see page 38).

The second part of the tune is measures 17-24 with a variation in measures 25-32. At this point, the tune has been established. Measures 33-48 are a variation on the first part, and measures 49-64 are variations on the second part. A low octave variation on the first part is in measures 65-80. Measures 81-96 present a third position variation on the first part. The fingerings should remain in third position through measure 94, changing to first position as the open string sounds. Note measure 85. This is a classic fiddle lick using the open E string with higher pitches sounding on the A string. Another variation on the second part is in measures 97-112. This is a very common variation idea, and this or something similar should be used in your own version. A final variation on the first part closes this arrangement in measures 113-128.

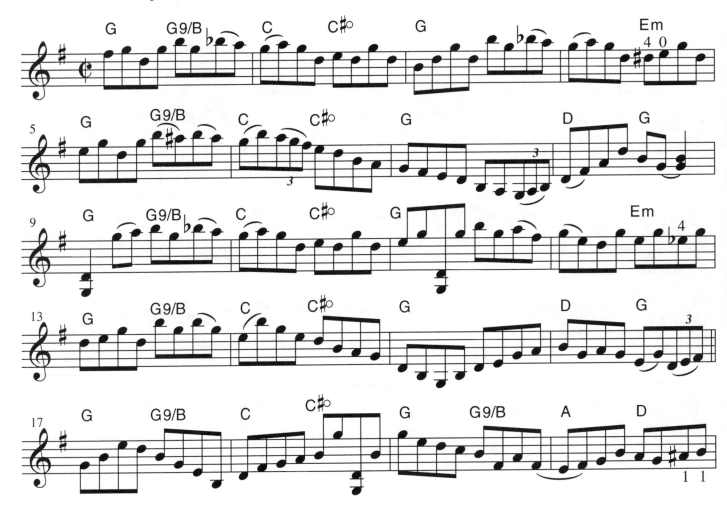

44

Variation - Part One

Variation - Part Two

45

Variation - Part One Low Octave

Variation - Part One Third Position

Variation - Part Two

Variation - Part One

47

Sally Goodin'

Sally Goodin' is a two-part tune played by square dance, old time, bluegrass and contest fiddlers. Although there are really only two parts, it is played with so many variations, that many of the variations have become standard parts of the tune. This is the basic melody.

In the above melody each part is four measures long and is repeated. In the following arrangement, each section has a written out repeat with a slight variation.

Square dance style bowings are indicated in this arrangement. A Texas contest style fiddler would use more separate "saw strokes," rarely using the shuffle bowings found in measures 1-15.

Measures 1-8 state the opening part using a fourth finger "A" on the D string as a drone. This should be practiced until it becomes very comfortable, as this is a very characteristic fiddling technique. Measures 9-16 state the second part continuing the use of the fourth finger and the open string being played together. The first part is varied in measures 17-24 with second finger slides and ryhthmic bowing.

48

A variation of the second part is found in measures 25-32. Notice how various bowings are used, including Georgia Bow. In measure 29, the bow should be heavy on the beats and very light on the second, third and fourth notes of the measure, almost "stuttering" over these three notes. A high octave variation on the first part uses third position fingerings in measures 33-40, with a return to first position as the open strings are played in measures 36 and 40. The next part is the first real diversion from the two original parts. It adds an F# to the downbeat of each measure, giving a 6th coloring to the chord and uses triplets throughout the section. Another variation of the first part, measures 49-56, uses first position with the fourth finger stretching for the C naturals and then sliding back to the B.

The extension of the fourth finger is continued in measures 57-64. The use of Georgia bow gives an off-beat rhythmic drive to this variation. Measure 65 starts in second position and uses quite a few slides. The slides should be understated. The slides in measures 66 and 70 are a "fall" and should not sound the entire distance between the pitches. This can be done by slightly taking the pressure off of the left-hand fingering as you move to the lower position. This section acts as a cue to the accompaniment that the minor section is next. Measures 73-80 change to F♯ minor, continuing to add variation to the first part of the tune. This section is repeated. Another variation on the first part is in measures 81-88.

Another variation on the second part is in measures 89-96. The sweeping triplets are characteristic of Texas style contest fiddling. The last quarter in measure 93 doubles the fourth finger and open E to create an accent. Measures 97, 99 and 101 are to be played with very short bow strokes on the first four eighth notes, followed by a full bow stroke on the dotted quarter. This same technique is used in measure 105. A final variation of the second part is in measures 105-112. The last four measures are a tag or ending and are not a part of the tune.

51

Westphalia Waltz

This is one of the most popular fiddle waltzes. It is played in contests as well as for dances and shows. The bowing should be very smooth and connected using long bow strokes. The bow is lifted during the eighth note rests in measures 33, 34, 49 and 50. This arrangement uses many fiddle style grace notes and double stops. The E grace note in measure 27 should be played on the beat, not before it. The chord changes in the second part, measures 33-64, are very pretty, however, the part is often played with much simpler chord changes.

52

This is another arrangement of *Westphalia Waltz*, showing additional variation ideas. More double stops are used, as well as a few more moving notes. The double stops are not essential, so the same licks may be played with single notes. The bowing is still smooth, connected, long strokes. Once again, the bow is lifted in measures 97, 98, 113 and 114 allowing the notes to ring through the rests. The last measure gives a typical ending.

Jolie Blonde

Jolie Blonde is the most popular Cajun waltz. Cajun waltzes are very rhythmic, frequently using a quarter-eighth-eighth-eighth-eighth bowing pattern in each measure. Double stops are used extensively in this style.

The first eight measures of this arrangement are written as single notes, to show the melody. However, they are typically played as double stops as indicated in the following eight measures. The tune is not always performed as a strict AB form. The vocal to the tune is only on the A part. The B section is part of the instrumental interlude and is usually included when *Jolie Blonde* is played as an instrumental.

The last measure on this page is a "final" measure and is to be omitted when the tune is repeated.

As in the previous version, the first measure is a pickup to the tune. Therefore, when this variation follows the first variation, the pickup measure takes the place of the last measure on the previous page.

Several Cajun licks are used in this version. The bowing is very rhythmic, as Cajun waltzes are energetic dance music. Double stops are used thoughout, often as open-string drones. The triplets and turns are very stylistic and can be used in other tunes played in this style. Note the shift in the third line to third finger. The fingerings indicated in the next measure make up a standard lick. The final two measures provide a typical ending.

55

Ashokan Farewell

Jay Ungar

Jay Ungar wrote this tune as a farewell piece for his fiddle camp. He recorded it in 1983 with the band *Fiddle Fever*. When PBS did the Civil War documentary with Ken Burns, this piece was chosen as the background music as letters from soldiers were read. It has such a plaintive melody, that it caught the ear of the American public and has been frequently requested since. Although it is not really a Civil War piece, because of its association with the documentary, it is often referred to as "that tune from the Civil War."

Unlike most American fiddle waltzes, this tune is played with even eighths, not swing eighths. In fact, the pick-ups and the rhythms is measures 1, 2, 8, 9 and 10 all use a Scottish fiddle rhythm of sixteenth - dotted eighth.

56

The original recording of *Ashoken Farewell* begins with unaccompanied fiddle. Later in the recording there are three fiddles playing the tune in harmony. Here are harmony parts you can play with other fiddlers.

The low harmony is the third fiddle part. If there are only two fiddlers, the high part should be played.

This double stop arrangement of *Ashoken Farewell* can be used by one fiddler to imply the harmonies of multiple fiddlers playing the tune. It can follow directly after the single string version. There are several challenging double stops, so it should be practiced very carefully so that each note is in tune.

The last time through the tune, the accompaniment stops on the C chord (as in measure 58) and does not play the next two measures. The fiddler can ritard or "stretch" this part and return to tempo when the accompaniment comes back in on the D chord (as in measure 61). The phrase in measures 61-64 is the standard ending for the tune.

Western Swing

In the 1940's, as "swing" music was booming across the country with the sounds of Glen Miller, Duke Elling-ton and other Big Band greats, country and western bands began playing in a similar style. Fiddler Bob Wills had the most successful of these bands, traveling across Texas and the west spreading the sounds of "Western Swing." These bands used fiddles as the main lead instrument, often having two or three fiddlers playing in harmony and trading solos. Some of the most famous tunes were *San Antonio Rose, Take Me Back to Tulsa, Stay All Night, Stay a Little Longer* and *Faded Love*. Here is the vocal for *Faded Love*.

Faded Love

By Bob Wills & Johnny Wills
vocal version

Verse

As I read the let-ters that you wrote to me, it is
As I think of the past and all the plea-sures we had, as I

you that I am think-ing of. As I
watch the mat-ing of the dove, It was

read the lines that to me were so sweet, I re-
in the spring-time that we said good-bye and I re-

mem - ber our fad - ed love. I
mem - ber our fad - ed love.

Chorus

miss you dar-ling more and more ev'-ry day, As

hea - ven would miss the stars a - bove. With

ev' - ry heart-beat I still think of you and re-

mem - ber our fad - ed love.

Although *Faded Love* is usually sung in the key of A, it is usually fiddled in the key of D. Following is an arrangement using swing style fiddle licks. The eighth notes are played with a swing feel (like a quarter note-eighth note triplet.) Most versions of *Faded Love* start with the fiddle in D, and modulate to A for the vocal, using D, D♯, E7 half note chords for the modulation. After the vocal, an A7 chord is used to modulate back to the key of D for the instrumental solo. This solo opens with three down bows, with a lift between each stroke. This is a common "country" fiddle beginning. Note also that the fourth finger doubles the open A. The grace notes all begin on the beat, not before it. The playing should be rhythmic, but relaxed with each note played precisely in tune on or just ever so slightly behind the beat. "Play it lazy" is a phrase often used to describe this feeling.

Track #31

Faded Love

By Bob Wills & Johnny Wills

fiddle melody

Faded Love - harmony one

Faded Love is a favorite tune for fiddlers to play in harmony. This harmony part is the part above the melody for the verse and changes to the part below the melody for the chorus, ending above the melody in the last measure and a half. The licks work well with the previous arrangement. Many of the turns and grace notes are still in place, although several have been omitted. It is not necessary to parallel every lick when playing harmonies. The opening movement from D to C♯ to C natural implies the chord changes of D, D major 7 to D7.

By Bob Wills & Johnny Wills

Faded Love - harmony two

This harmony part is to be used when there are three fiddlers. It uses less of the grace notes, giving the ensemble a smoother sound and allowing the melody to stand out. The verse harmony is one part below the melody. The chorus harmony is two parts below the melody, acting as a low tenor part, until the final measure and a half. The D, D major 7 to D7 chord progresson is implied in the first part of the chorus.

By Bob Wills & Johnny Wills

Maiden's Prayer

This traditional tune is often associated with Bob Wills and Western Swing. It is a one-part tune played in a swing 4/4 time. The basic melody is found in measures 1-16. The pickups are down bow chops, lifting between each stroke. Fiddlers often use this bowing lick to set the tempo without audibly counting the tune off. After the pickups, the bowing should be very smooth and connected, using long strokes. The eighth notes are all played as swing eighths (quarter - eighth triplets.) Measures 17- 64 contain three additional variations to the tune.

The second time through offers rhythmic variation as well as fiddle style double stops. Keep the rhythm very relaxed as you play through the pushes into measures 20, 22, and 24. The slide in measure 24 from the C# down to the C natural should be treated as a blues note.

The first two lines of this variation are played tremolo. Try starting softly and getting louder and then softer again as indicated. Be certain to place the second and third fingers close enough together in measure 38, so that they are in tune. This double stop using the third and seventh of the chord is useful in many fiddling applications. Measures 33-40 are also very effective played without the tremolo. Yet another variation on the ascending line is in measures 41-44. The final phrase appears an octave higher in measures 44-48. The high E is played as a harmonic and the shifts are done as the open E string sounds.

The adding of a sixth to a chord is a characteristic sound of Western Swing. An A6 chord (A,C♯,E,F♯) is used in measures 49, 50, 57 and 58. A D6 chord (D,F♯,A,B) is used in measures 52 and 60. The half step slides are also typical. The bowing should be slightly separated in measures 49 and 57 on the quarter notes. Otherwise it is connected and should really swing. The shifts to third position take place as the open strings sound in measures 50, 52, 58 and 60.

Irish/Celtic Music

The popularity of Irish and Celtic music has spread world wide. This traditional music comes from Ireland, Scotland, Wales, England and Normandy. It is also played widely in Canada, Australia and here in the United States. It is primarily dance music including jigs, reels, hornpipes and airs.

The melody is the most important part of this tradition. In fact, collections of the tunes such as *O'Neill's Music of Ireland* and J. Scott Skinner's *The Scottish Violinist* do not contain chord symbols. Fiddlers, pipers, flute and tin whistle players and other musicians all play the melody together. The melodies, therefore are more consistent from player to player. The theme and variation form of Old Time and Bluegrass music does not exist here. What does exist is an extensive use of ornamentation. Fiddlers use both fingering and bowing ornaments. As the music is played together, different instruments will use varying ornaments at the same time, but it all works within the style.

In recent years, traditional percussion has been added to the music along with guitars and bouzoukis. The Irish bouzouki is an eight string instrument sounding one octave lower than a mandolin. There are also many recordings using modern instrumentation with bass, electric guitars and electronic keyboards. This updates the traditional tunes to fit within today's musical climate, however, the melody remains the most important part.

Jigs

The jig is one of the most popular types of Celtic tunes. It is a dance tune in 6/8, played at a medium to fast tempo. There are two beats per measure, with a feeling of three to each beat. When the measure is counted, an accent falls on the first and fourth eighth note (1 2 3 4 5 6.) A tune in 9/8 is a "slip jig." It has three beats per measure with an accent on the first, fourth and seventh eighth note (1 2 3 4 5 6 7 8 9.) Occasionally there are tunes written in 6/8 that are played very slowly, such *Sheebeg, Sheemore* and *Fanny Power*. Although these tunes are technically slow jigs, they feel more like waltzes.

Track #33

Irish Washerwoman

This is the most popular jig played in the United States. It is not found in *O'Neill's Music of Ireland* and I have heard that it is in fact an English tune. It appears in *M.M.Coles One Thousand Fiddle Tunes* as *Irish Wash Woman Jig*. In that version the E in the third measure is a D, so the Am chord would become a D7. The entire tune is often played with no slurs. The bowing emphasis in jigs is usually on the beat.

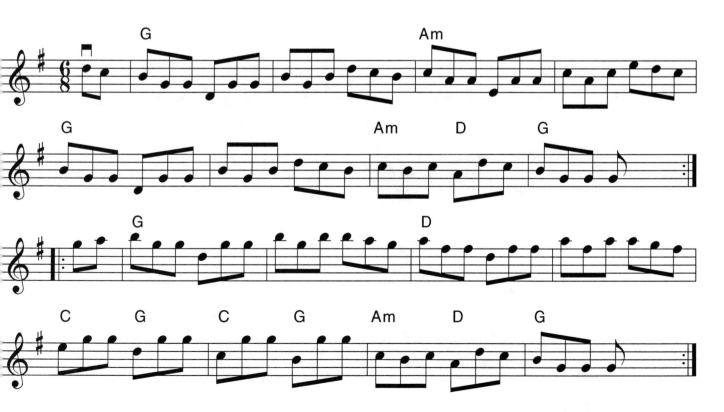

65

Swallowtail Jig

This is a traditional jig in E minor, using a common chordal theme of going back and forth between a minor chord and the major chord a whole step below it. The bowing should accent the beat.

Celtic tunes are frequently played through three times, and are often combined with other tunes in the same style. These medleys are called sets. They can be two, three or more tunes long, and in varying keys. *Swallowtail Jig* makes a very nice set with *Irish Washerwoman*.

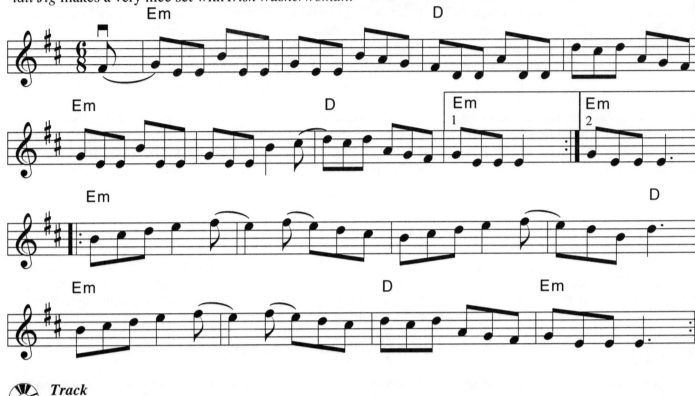

Track #34

Here is the same tune with a few embellishments added. The first part remains the same except for an added sixteenth in the sixth measure. The second part makes extensive use of the first to third finger turn. In classical music, grace note turns are usually to the note above. This is common in Irish music, but it is also common for notes that fall on a first finger, to use a turn going up to the third finger.

Garry Owen

General George Custer used this as a march tune for the Seventh Calvary. There is also a traditional Irish song written to this tune about some rogues from the town of Garryowen in County Limerick. In the song the last measure ends on a G. However, the usual practice when played as an instrumental is to end each part on the D chord. The last measure written here, which ends on a G, is only used for the final measure after all repeats of the tune.

Although Celtic tunes are not played in a theme and variation form, it is common to play the melody in different octaves, particularly when playing with several instruments. *Garry Owen* works very well in the low octave.

The Kesh Jig

This tune has been recorded by several Irish groups including *The Bothy Band* and *Boys of the Lough*. It is a beautiful tune that really shines with the proper embellishment. Here is the unadorned melody.

Rolls

When notes are repeated in Irish tunes, such as in the first measure, it is common practice to play a grace note between the repeated notes. This comes from imitating the pipes which can not repeat a note. When there is enough time, or there are three repeated notes, it is stylistic to play a roll as indicated in the first and last measures of this arrangement. Notice the use of the first to third finger grace notes in the second measure. They have been combined into another type of roll common in Irish fiddling found several times in this arrangement.

Track #36

Haste to the Wedding

This traditional Irish tune is a favorite among fiddlers and penny whistle players. The bowing accents the beat. It is usually played at a medium fast tempo although I have heard it played as a lilting waltz.

This version of *Haste to the Wedding* gives several examples of left-hand embellishment. The first to third finger grace note is used in measures 2, 6 and 14. The other embellishments use neighboring and connecting tones. Notice the bowing adds slurs to make the grace notes smooth, but still keep the emphasis on the beat. Learn to play these turns and experiment with adding embellishments of your own.

Track #37

Morrison's Jig

Irish fiddler, James Morrison recorded this tune on a Columbia studio recording in 1936. He called the tune *Maurice Carmody's Favourite*, but it is better known today as *Morrison's Jig*. It makes extensive use of the roll, indicated by the mordant symbol in the first part. The mordant means to play E-F♯-E-D-E in the space of the dotted quarter. It is also stylistic to use a G instead of an F♯ in the roll. The B's in measures 1, 2, 5 and 6 should be slightly accented, emphasizing the 2 against 3 rhythm. The second part is not repeated, as it is twice as long as the first part and contains somewhat of a built-in repeat. The accents in this part are all on the beat. The C chord in the next to last measure of the tune has come into common use, although the Em is more traditional. When the C chord is used, the third note is played as a C natural instead of a C sharp. After all repetitions of the tune it ends on the Em.

The rolls are written out in this version of *Morrison's Jig*. The bowing should accent the string crossings in the first part, and the beat throughout. The seventh and eighth measures of the second part should be played with emphasis on the down beat. A few embellishments have also been added to the second part.

Track
#38

D.C.   last time only

Merrily Kiss the Quaker

This tune is not in *O'Neill's Music of Ireland* or *Howe's 1000 Jigs and Reels* or any of my other traditional sources, so I'm not certain of it's origin. Several Irish bands have recorded the tune, including *The Boys of the Lough, Planxty* and *The Chieftains*. It is a three part tune which is quite fun to play.

This is the unadorned tune with a few bowings added. The first two parts begin with a down bow slur into the downbeat. There should be a slight accent on the second note of these slurs. The last part begins up bow even though the preceeding part ends up bow. Just stop the bow briefly and continue up bow, making it sound as if you changed direction. This keeps the down bow on the beat, properly emphasizing the rhythm.

The most important thing about bowing is to give the proper accent and lilt to the tune. This version of *Merrily Kiss the Quaker* begins up bow, since the remaining bowings work better this way. Measures 2, 4 and 6 use a bowing of down bow on the first third of the beat and up bow on the remaining two thirds of the beat. This gives a real lilt to the beat. The turns indicated are very typical ornaments, particularly the roll on the repeated notes in the last measure of each part. When playing a roll, such as these ending measures and measures 1, 3 and 4 of the third part, it is stylistic to hold the first note a little longer than an eighth note, and then do a fast turn.

Track #39

73

The Road to Lisdoonvarna

This is a well-known jig from western Ireland. Once again we have a tune based on the chodal pattern of a minor chord (Em) alternating with the major chord (D) one step below. This is the unadorned melody.

Snap Bowing

Celtic tunes frequently use a bowing embellishment known as "snap bowing." The name describes the technique involved. The first note of the lick is "snapped" quickly with a bit of tension in the bow hand. The tension is immediately released as the bow springs back and forth on the notes to follow. Sometimes three notes are played and sometimes four are played. The bowing may also be combined with grace notes as in measure 5.

Track #40

Maggie Brown's Favorite

This traditional tune is often played at a slower pace than the typical jig. In *The Chieftains'* recording of the tune, the first part is not repeated, although it is repeated in several written sources. The second part is not repeated. The two slurs indicated are there to keep the down bows on the down beat.

The embellishments in this arrangement of *Maggie Brown's Favorite* all come on the repeated notes of the unadorned melody. There are rolls in measures 2, 4, 6 and 8 of the first part. The repeat has been omitted. The second measure of the second part has a snap bowing embellishment. This lick is interchangeable with the left-hand turn lick four measures later. The bowing throughout the tune is indicated to keep the accent on the beat, using down bows on the down beats.

 Track #41

The Blarney Pilgrim

This is one of my favorite jigs. It is found in *O'Neill's Music of Ireland* as well as other traditional sources. The tune is in D mixolydian mode. The mixolydian mode is the same as a major scale, but with a flat seventh scale degree. In others words, in the key of D mixolydian, a C natural is used instead of a C sharp. Many Irish tunes use this mode.

Here is the melody of the tune without embellishments. A few bowings are marked, to make it flow smoothly. The beat should be very strong. In particular, the quarter notes in the first, second, fifth and sixth measures of the third part should be accented.

The bowings in the first and fifth measures of this embellished arrangement really emphasize the beat. This pattern of down bow for one eighth note followed by up bow for two eighth notes is a very effective jig bowing. Snap bowing is used in measures 3, 4, 7, 15, 19 and 20. In each of these cases, the lick starts up bow and slurs out of the lick up bow. The first note of the snap is heavier than the second and third notes. This technique is a stylistic embellishment and should not sound as an even triplet. The third part begins with the bow playing a double stop on the string crossings. This is also a powerful effect emphasizing the beat.

All of the embellished versions of tunes in this book present fiddling concepts and techniques. The arrangements are not intended to be definitive versions of each tune, but are intended to give an understanding of fiddling styles. These ideas should be learned and incorporated into other tunes.

Track #42

Reels

Reels are dance tunes that have two beats per measure with each beat divided into four parts. They are usually played at a fast tempo. They may be written in Cut Time or in 2/4. Many of the tunes played as breakdowns and square dance tunes are also reels.

Miss McLeod's Reel

This reel with a Scottish name is played in Scotland and Ireland and throughout North America. It has several titles including *Hop Light, Ladies* and *Did You Ever See the Devil?* As indicated, the final measure is not played until the tunes ends. This is the straight forward version.

In the following version, the first part uses a grace note or a "cut" between the repeated notes in measures 2, 4 and 6. This technique is used by pipers and pennywhistle players, so it is imitated by fiddlers. The second part makes extensive use of the first finger turn. Some players reverse the order of the parts, particularly if they are playing the tune as *Hop Light, Ladies*.

Track #43

The Girl I Left Behind Me

Although this is a rather simple tune, it is played by celtic, oldtime and contradance fiddlers. I have heard it in old western movies in barndance scenes and I have heard it sung with Irish lyrics. This is the basic melody.

The ornamentation in this version is in a celtic, rather than an old time style. There is a regular turn in the first measure, a first to third finger turn in the second and a roll in the last measure of each part. The bowing is quite varied, using saw strokes, then slurring into beats, and later using three note slurs. All of these techniques are used to bring life to the tune.

Track
#44

The Rakes of Mallow

This Irish tune is also the melody for a song. It is a catchy, simple melody, so it is good for ensemble playing. Placing an accent on the offbeat in measures 1, 3, and 5 give a lilt to the tune.

Although the tune is usually played in G, it also works well in D. This is also a better key for the vocal version. The first part may also be played up an octave.

81

Red Haired Boy
The Little Beggarman

The Little Beggarman is an Irish song using the same melody as this tune. The bowing style in this arrangement changes direction every half beat. This is an unusual pattern that gives a lilt to the tune as each stroke is lightly accented.

Some versions of the tune go to the G chord on the down beat of the fourth measure instead of the second bea When this is the case, the first two notes of measure four are B A.

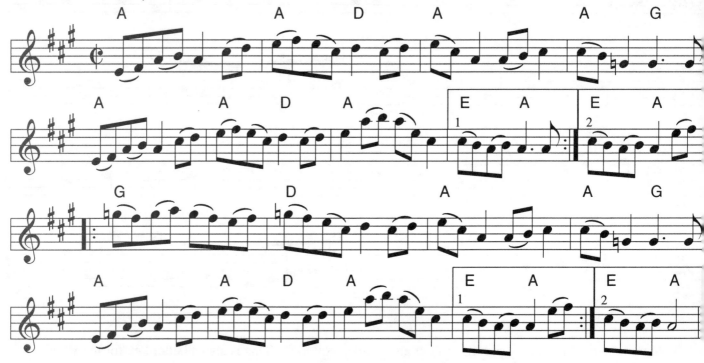

Red Haired Boy Harmony

This makes a good twin fiddle tune. Here is the high harmony using the same style bowing. The beginning of the second part works best in second position, shifting back to first position while the open E is being played.

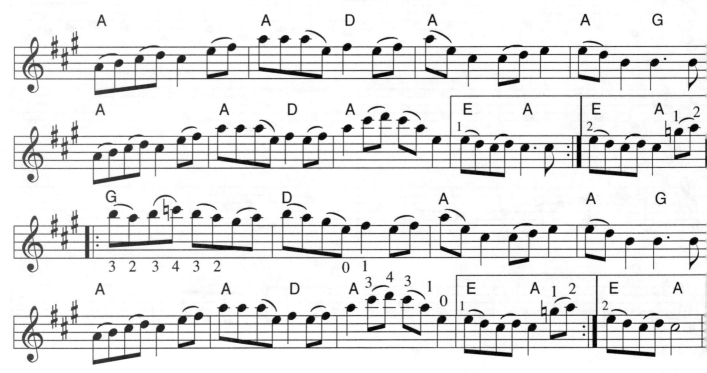

Guilderoy

This is almost the same tune as *Red Haired Boy,* played in a minor mode. It is a contradance tune found in *Howe's 1000 Jigs and Reels* (ca. 1867.) Except for the occasional G♯, it is in the Dorian mode. The Dorian mode is a scale with minor third, major sixth and minor seventh scale degrees. Many Irish tunes are in this mode. The bowings are suggestions. In fact, I would most likely play the pickup notes down-up and use the slur on the repeat.

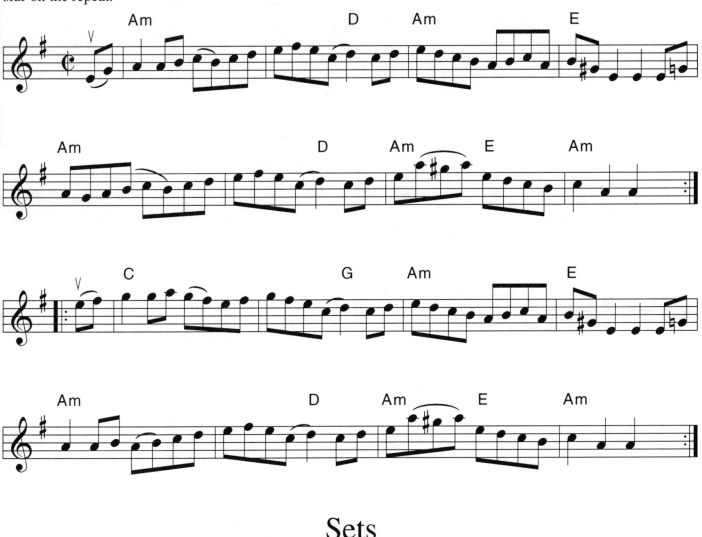

Sets

Just like jigs, reels are often played in sets of two, three or more tunes. The usual format is for each tune to be played through three times, then to go directly to the next tune. The tunes may be in the same key or the keys may vary. This type of set is common practice in Irish pubs and on traditional celtic recordings. *Guilderoy* and *Red Haired Boy* make a very nice set, beginning in the minor mode with *Guilderoy* and ending in the major mode with *Red Haired Boy*.

Another type of set consists of tunes in different styles. A commonly used combination is a waltz or air, followed by a jig, followed by a reel. In this type of set, the tunes are not necessarily played three times each. In fact, it is more usual for the slow tune to be played once, and the following tunes twice. These sets are used mainly for shows and contests, as the tempos increase from tune to tune.

St. Anne's Reel

Played by celtic, Irish, oldtime and bluegrass musicians, this is a Canadian tune. There are many versions of the melody and the chords. This version has the traditional chords and is in the Canadian style of fiddling, with arppegiated chords as the licks throughout the first part. The bowing is mostly saw stroke. Notice the slur on the last two notes. This is a commonly used device to set up the down bow for the repeat.

The fiddling of Howdy Forrester of Tennessee inspired this arrangement. His version uses a C natural in the third and fourth measures of the first part. The chords in the second part were not in his version, but have come into common usage. The Bm is in parenthesis because it is an optional substitution for the D chord. The bowing in this version is more of an oldtime fiddling style. The first and fifth measures of the second part use a down bow on the E string followed by three up bows on the A, emphasizing the rhythm with the string crossings.

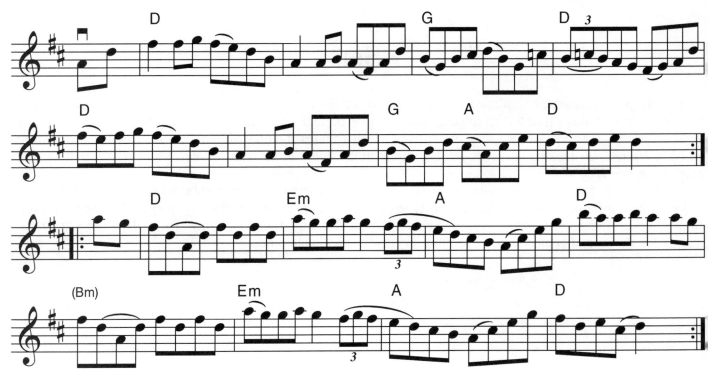

Temperance Reel

This is a two part reel centering around G and E minor. It is a traditional tune played by fiddlers from varied backgrounds. The basic melody is presented here. Some musicians use the same notes in the fourth measure of the second part as are in the second and sixth measures of the second part (see alternate B part.) I prefer the first option for two reasons. The first is that these notes fit the chord changes better and the second is that varying the lick is more interesting than using the same lick three times.

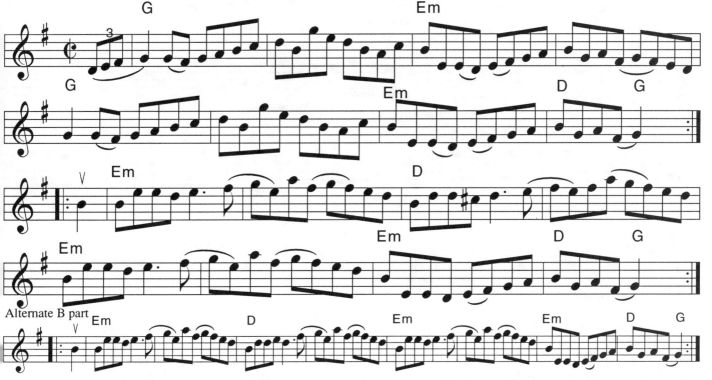

This is a typical way *Temperence Reel* is ornamented. The rolls in the first part are very much a part of the tune. The bowing in the first, third and fifth measures of the second part should emphasize the beat, with very short strokes on the repeated E's and D's.

Track #49

Flowers of Edinburgh

This is a two-part Scottish reel that is a favorite among many fiddlers. Here is the basic melody.

There are many ways to embellish this tune. The opening lick uses a combination of the snap bow and the triplet. The snap bow begins up bow, so there is a slur beginning on the third note, which is the first note of the triplet. In the first measure of the second line, the snap begins down bow, so the slur is one note later. The turns and the bowings may be varied in many ways in the second part. The embellishments in this version should be learned and then applied to this and other tunes to give them a true celtic flair.

Track #50

Drowsy Maggie

The title of this tune is very deceiving, as it is usually played quite fast. It has been recorded by a number of Irish groups including the *Chieftains*. Notice that the first part is eight measures long without a repeat and the second part is eight measures long and is repeated. Some versions of the tune do not repeat the second part, going directly to the second ending. The chord changes are not a standard thing in Irish music, and vary from version to version of the same tune. The Bm in the endings of this version is often played as an Em. Here is the melody without embellishments.

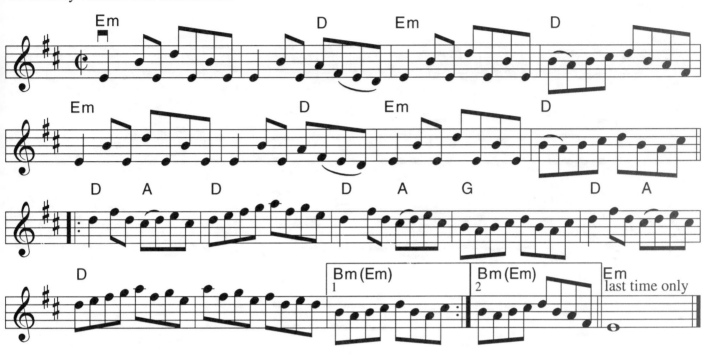

The first part of the following arrangement uses a slide up to the opening pitch. The turns and grace notes are very stylistic. The bowing in the second part works well to add emphasis to the offbeat and still give a smooth flow.

Track
#51

The Pigeon on the Gate

This is a traditional Irish reel found in *O'Neill's Music of Ireland* and recorded by several famous Irish fiddlers including Kevin Burke. This version uses the snap bowing as a key feature in the first part. The bowings indicated in measures 1, 2, 5 and 6 help set up the snap bowing. The "E's" in the first and fifth measures of the second part should be played with the fourth finger as indicated to make the tune flow smoothly. *The Pigeon on the Gate* and *Drowsy Maggie* make a very nice set of tunes, played in the same key and with the same attitude.

Scotland the Brave

Not only is this a great fiddling tune, it is THE song to stir Scottish patriotism. It is played at a fast march tempo. When the song is sung, the parts are not repeated, so even when played as an instrumental the repeats are optional. Some fiddlers play the tune in the key of G, but D is best for vocal range.

Scotland the Brave - Key of G

Scotland the Brave (vocal)

Hark when the night is fal - ling Hear, hear the pipes are cal - ling
Out by the mis - ty high - lands, Down by the pur - ple is - lands,

Loud - ly and proud - ly fal - ling down through the glen. Now feel your heart a beat - ing,
Brave are the hearts that beat be - neath Scot - tish skies. Wild are the winds that meet you,

Now feel your spi - rit leap - ing High as the spi - rits of the old hill men.
Staunch are the friends that greet you, High as the love that shines in fair maid - en's eye.

Torn and gal - lant fame, Scot - land my moun - tain hame. High may your proud ban - ners

glo - ri - ous - ly wave. Land of my high en - dea - vor, land of the shi - ning ri - ver,

Land of my heart for - e - ver, Scot - land the Brave.

The Salamanca Reel

This is a fine Irish reel that has been recorded by a number of musicians including *The Bothy Band*. It contains a number of triplet turns which are part of the tune itself. The slurs into the second beat of the seventh and eighth measures and in the second part are very stylistic, breaking up the constant eighth note bowing pattern.

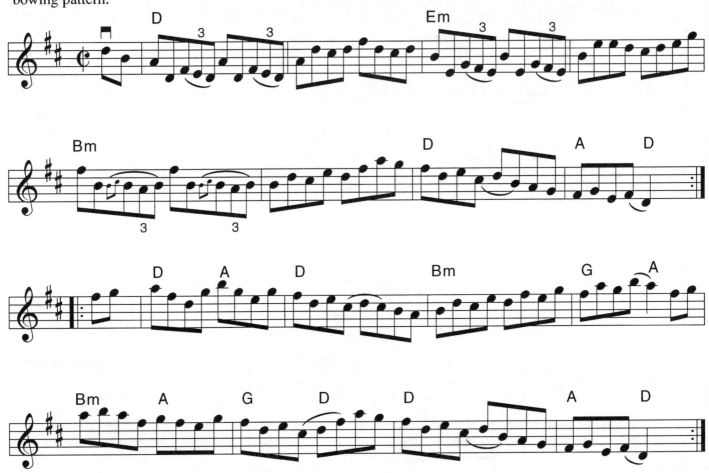

This is the first part with the same notes but with slightly different bowings and turns. The bowing in the first line allows the left hand to do the ornaments as the right hand accents the beat. The turns before the triplets in the fifth measure use the first to third finger turn instead of the grace note indicated above.

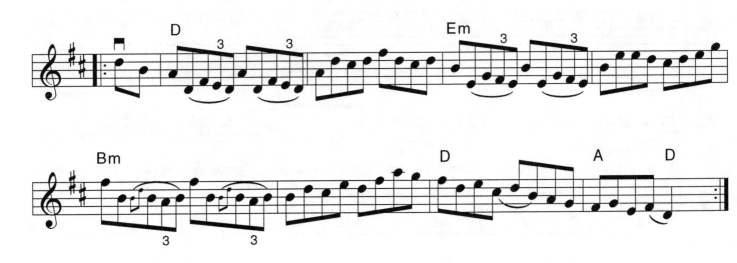

Hornpipes

Hornpipes, like reels have two beats per measure and are written in cut time. The major difference is that hornpipes are played with a swing feel where sometimes the beat is divided into four parts and sometimes into three. Hornpipes are generally slower than reels. In the Irish tradition, hornpipes are tunes that are used for hard shoe step dancing, in which the dancers tap out very intricate rhythms. In bluegrass and old time circles, tunes like *Fisher's Hornpipe* and *Sailor's Hornpipe* are played with even eighths, more like reels or old time square dance tunes.

Track #55

Harvest Home

This tune is played by fiddlers throughout Scotland, Ireland and other hot spots of celtic music. It is performed at a medium slow tempo. The triplet lick in measure four is varied in the second part, as found in J. Scott Skinner's *The Scottish Violinist*. However, many fiddlers use the first lick in both parts.

The first two measures of the second part are often played as follows.

91

The Rights of Man

This traditional Irish hornpipe is not found in many sources of Irish fiddle tunes, although it has been recorded by famous musicians including the group *De Danann*. Hornpipes are often written as even eighth notes with the understanding that the player knows to swing the rhythm. This arrangement uses dotted rhythms to make certain the hornpipe feel is used. Notice the D grace notes in the first part. These add a real Irish flair to the tune. The slurs into the grace notes give an added emphasis.

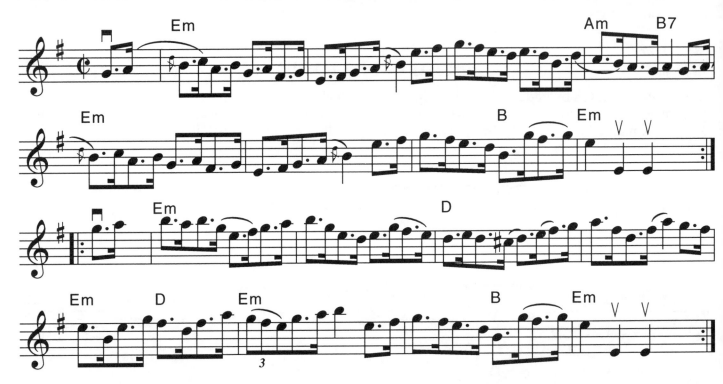

Triplets are added to the opening measure of this arrangement as well as to the final phrase. A slur has been added into the last measure of each part. The slurs in the second part are also different. Bowing may be varied in many ways as long as the style and rhythm of the tune are emphasised.

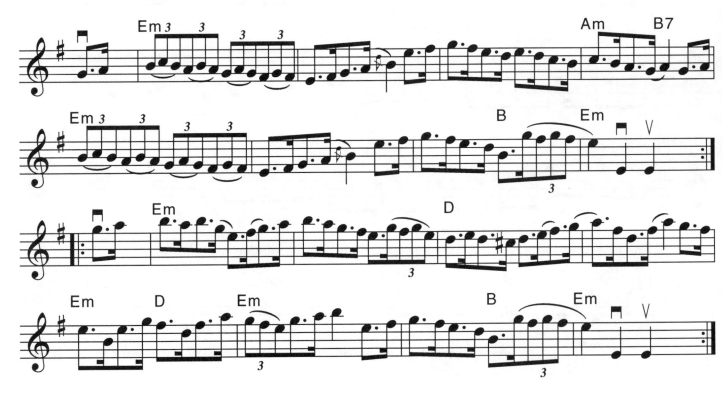

Airs

The slow tempo tunes in celtic music are called airs. They may be waltzes, or may be in other time signatures. There are marching airs in Scottish music, but most are beautiful melodies that should be played with emotion. Airs are often played very slowly, without the feeling of a strict tempo. The notes should be very connected, with long smooth bow strokes. Vibrato should be used, but not a classical sounding vibrato. It should be relatively slow and very easy. Airs are delicate tunes and should be performed in a delicate manner.

Track *#57*

Gentle Maiden

This very beautiful tune comes from the Irish tradition. I have also heard it called *Gentle Maid*. Although it is written in 6/8, it is performed very slowly, giving it the feel of a waltz. I enjoy playing tunes like this without accompaniment on the opening two lines, having the other musicians join in in the ninth measure. This entire tune can then be repeated with various instruments as needed.

The first two measures of the third line contain several repeated notes. The only way Irish bagpipes can repeat a note is to play other notes between the repeated ones. Fiddlers often copy this style. Here is an example of how this works on these two measures.

93

Give Me Your Hand

Tabhair Dom Do Lamh

Ruainn Dall O Cathain wrote this beautiful melody. The original Gaelic name is Tabhair Dom Do Lamh. The tune is writtten here to be played twice through with a two measure ending added after the repeat. The tune is written in 6/8, but is performed with the feel of a medium fast waltz. The bowing should be very smooth and connected. The D on the downbeat of the tenth measure may also be played down an octave. It is stylistic to add grace notes between repeated notes, however, it should not be overdone.

94

Turlough O Carolan

The most famous of all Irish composers was an itinerant harpist who lived from 1670-1738. He caught smallpox when he was 18 years old and it left him blind. He then began the study of the harp and his traveling career began three years later. His playing was not particularly good, in fact he was scorned by his fellow harpists. The first house he visited was owned by George Reynolds of County Leitrim. Mr. Reynolds advised him that he "might make a better hand of his tongue than his fingers." After this comment, Carolan wrote his first song, *Si Bheag, Si Mhor* to the tune of *The Bonnie Cuckoo*. Following this composition, he continued to write throughout his life. Many of his compositions were written in honor of his patrons or their relatives. He would compose a piece while traveling, and add lyrics after the tune was complete. His lyrics have been lost over the span of time, but his melodies still hold a prominent place in Irish music.

Track #58

Fanny Power

This composition was written in honor of Miss Fanny Power. It is one of three tunes written for the Power family, the others being *David Power* and *Mrs. Power* or *Carolan's Concerto*. Although it is in 6/8, it is played as a waltz. The bowing should be very smooth and connected. The slurs indicated are suggestions to achieve this sound. The repeats are optional. Carolan's compositions have survived as one line melodies, so any chord changes are all modern additions. The descending bass line in the second part is my own version.

Si Bheag, Si Mhor
Sheebeg, Sheemore

This is the first song Carolan wrote. The lyric was based on a legend about a war between two fairy armies.
A loose translation of the title is "*Little Fairy Hill, Big Fairy Hill*." The tune is played widely in celtic circles.
It was originally written in 6/8, but is performed as a waltz. The repeats are optional. One performance
possibility is to play the repeats the first time through the tune and then play the second time without repeats.